Edward
the "Crazy Man"

Annick Press Ltd.
All rights reserved. No part of this work covered by the copyrights hereon may be reproduced or used in any form or by any means – graphic, electronic, or mechanical – without the prior written permission of the publisher.

We acknowledge the support of the Canada Council for the Arts, the Ontario Arts Council, and the Government of Canada through the Book Publishing Industry Development Program (BPIDP) for our publishing activities.

Cataloging in Publication Data

Day, Marie
    Edward the "Crazy man"

ISBN 1-55037-721-3 (bound).—ISBN 1-55037-720-5 (pbk.)

    1. Schizophrenia—Juvenile fiction. I. Title.

PS8557.A94E39 2002   jC813'.54   C2001-902837-7
PZ7.D3318Ed 2002

The art in this book was rendered in mixed media.
The text was typeset in Cochin Roman.

Distributed in Canada by:
Firefly Books Ltd.
3680 Victoria Park Avenue
Willowdale, ON
M2H 3K1

Published in the U.S.A. by:
Annick Press (U.S.) Ltd.
Distributed in the U.S.A. by:
Firefly Books (U.S.) Inc.
P.O. Box 1338, Ellicott Station
Buffalo, NY 14205

Printed and bound in Canada by Friesens, Altona, Manitoba.

visit us at: www.annickpress.com

For information on Schizophrenia, contact your local chapter of the Schizophrenia Society of Canada, the National Alliance for the Mentally Ill in the USA, or the National Schizophrenia Fellowship in the United Kingdom.

For beautiful, brave Naomi—M.D.

Special thanks to Dr Jorge Soni and Rick Wilks.

Edward
the "Crazy Man"

by
Marie Day

Annick Press Ltd.

Toronto ☆ New York ☆ Vancouver

"Would you look at that crazy man?" said Big Red, the crossing guard near Charlie's school. Charlie stood on tiptoe to see, but all he got was a glimpse of someone pushing a baby carriage through the busy traffic.

The very next morning, when Charlie took the shortcut through a lane, he suddenly came face to face with a man piling junk into a battered baby carriage. Charlie jumped a mile and so did the stranger. The man was wearing a fantastic costume made from an old curtain decorated with green plastic and shiny bits of silver foil. Charlie marveled at the magical way it was put together.

As Charlie stood staring, the man
spun his carriage around and rattled
off in a great hurry.

Charlie only got a quick look at his
eyes. They were bright blue and they
seemed to glitter like stars.

After that, Charlie spotted the man in all sorts of places. He would appear out of nowhere, always wearing costumes concocted from things people had thrown away.

There was all sorts of junk in Charlie's garage. He carefully selected items he thought the man might like to use to make costumes. Then, just after dark, he snuck into the lane and left them there.

The following day, Charlie was in the group being herded across the street by Big Red when all at once there was a lot of honking and yelling.

"Look! Crazy Man's at it again," said Big Red, heaving a great sigh.

Striding down the middle of the road came the man, ignoring all the angry drivers as usual. What a sight he was! He had used Charlie's presents to make a beautiful costume.

Charlie was almost
too excited to breathe.

"That guy's bananas," one of Charlie's schoolmates announced. It was Jake, the class bully. "Only a nutcase would dress up and parade around trying to get attention. My dad says weirdos like him should be put in straitjackets and locked up in a funny farm for good."

"That's a really dumb thing to say," blurted Charlie.

Then Jake stepped forward and gave him such a
punch in the stomach that Charlie was knocked
backwards into the zooming traffic. Just as he was
falling, someone snatched him out of the path of a
speeding car.

"Charlie! Are you alright?" Big Red asked anxiously. "You were almost run over."

"I'm OK," replied Charlie, jumping to his feet. "Thank you."

"Don't thank me, thank him," said Big Red, pointing to Crazy Man. "He saved your life."

But before Charlie could thank him, Crazy Man had dodged past the traffic and disappeared from sight.

That night Charlie's mom made him spaghetti, his favorite dinner. Afterwards, Charlie got out his colored pencils and drew a picture of Crazy Man. When he went to sleep, Charlie had a dream about him.

But Crazy Man never showed up again. No one knew his name or where he lived or what had become of him.

When he grew up, Charlie became a famous costume designer. He worked in a big building where sewing machines hummed all day as people put together new creations. He often wondered whatever happened to Crazy Man, with his wonderful costumes and his carriage full of junk.

Late one afternoon when Charlie was walking home, he noticed a homeless man huddled in a doorway. The man looked straight past him. His blue eyes glittered like stars. Charlie knew it was Crazy Man.

Charlie fished out one of his business cards and wrote on the back,

'I would like to help you – trust me.'

He placed the card in the man's lap and hurried on.

Weeks later, Charlie was in the middle of a costume fitting when a police officer arrived.

"We found a homeless man in really bad shape," she said. "We took him to the hospital. Your business card was in his pocket. You offered to help him. Is this true?"

"Yes," said Charlie. "That man saved my life!"

"Then go to the hospital and ask for Dr. Singh," said the officer.

Charlie grabbed his old drawing of Crazy Man, tucked it under his arm and headed off to the hospital.

Dr. Singh explained that the homeless man had a very serious illness that affects the brain. He thanked Charlie for coming.

He took Charlie to meet "Edward," for that was Crazy Man's real name. When he saw Charlie's drawing, Edward grinned and said, "I remember that outfit. The silver paint was still wet on those roses when I wore it."

"That day I was almost hit by a car and you saved my life," said Charlie. "Now I can finally thank you. I know what beautiful costumes you can make. When you are well, please come and work at my costume company."

It was months before Edward was discharged from the hospital. Because of his illness, he kept hearing voices in his head, and even with the best medication available, it was hard to act "normal." People usually shunned him.

One morning Charlie's secretary came into his office and whispered, "There is someone waiting to see you. His name is Edward. Says you know him."

"Send him right in," said Charlie.

Charlie was shocked to see how shabby Edward looked.

"Can you give me some work, Charlie? Things are rough," he said.

"Of course I can," said Charlie. "I told you I would, didn't I?"

All Edward did was decorate his hat with flowers made from scraps while he talked to himself in a loud voice. He sat away from the others and never spoke to anyone but Charlie. Charlie wasn't surprised when he overheard someone say, "Who's going to tell the boss to get rid of that weirdo?"

One morning a very famous rock star named Krackerjack came bounding into Charlie's office with his manager in tow. Krackerjack looked anxious while his manager did the talking.

"We've got a big problem. Krackerjack's luggage disappeared on a flight back from Australia. All his costumes are missing. He has nothing to wear for tonight's concert. We need something extravagant! Flamboyant! Unique! What can you show us? We're desperate!"

"Nothing, really. We do ballets and operas and musicals. I've never designed for rock concerts," Charlie explained.

"I want to look just like that," said Krackerjack, jerking a finger towards Charlie's drawing of Crazy Man. "Make me that!"

Charlie was about to say "Sorry," but then he had a brainwave.

"Wait here. I know who can do it," he said and rushed into the workroom, heading straight for Edward. As Charlie explained what was needed, Edward smiled and nodded, "Yes."

Edward quickly selected fabrics from the big shelves. He spread the cloth on the cutting table. Snip, snip went the scissors as Edward skillfully cut the patterns for a sleek costume of brilliant colors.

"How about giving me a hand?" Edward said to the others, who sat watching him in amazement. Everyone pitched in and worked feverishly to put Krackerjack's costume together in record time.

That night, Charlie and Edward went to the concert. Everyone cheered when Krackerjack burst onstage. Charlie could see that Edward felt very proud of the wonderful costume he had created for the famous rock star.

Next morning an E-mail arrived for Edward.

"Dear Edward, Thanks for that 'CRAZY' costume. I'll be starting
a world tour soon and I'll need a dozen new costumes. Will you
design them for me, please? I won't take no for an answer!"
Signed, Krackerjack

Edward said YES!

And he began dreaming up fantastic new creations that very day.

I used to design costumes, just like Charlie. It was fun to dream up creations for fictitious characters like Anne of Green Gables  or the haughty Princess Turandot,   or Hamlet.

But when a person I love got very sick I didn't have the heart to design costumes any more. Things are better now.

One day I saw a man dancing down the road wearing a cloak of green and orange plastic garbage bags. **A crazy man!** He was the inspiration for this book about Edward who suffers from a brain disease called schizophrenia and Charlie, who helps him.

I don't know if Edward designed more costumes for Krackerjack. I hope so. Maybe you, dear reader, know what happened. And please send me pictures of the costumes!

Marie Day

Send your pictures to Marie Day, c/o Annick Press Ltd. 15 Patricia Avenue, Toronto, ON. M2M 1H9